BILLIONAIRE'S TEMPTATION

L. STEELE

1

Edward

I stab the needle into my vein. Depress the plunger and the transparent substance sinks into my blood. Even before I've pulled out the syringe and sunk onto the dusty floor of the drug den, the numbness kicks in.

It always follows the same path. Up my toes, my feet, my calves, my knees, my thighs, my hips, my chest, shoulders and finally… Finally, the thoughts swirling around in my head quieten. Silence descends, a hazy, swirling fog that clears to reveal the most beautiful scene ever. I am on the beach, walking at the edge of the water. My feet sink into the powdery, soft sand which clings to my toes with every step I take. The waves swoop in, splash across my feet, pull away, leaving them clean.

If only I could wipe my past with such little effort. Erase everything that happened. Rub out... Remove, obliterate, eliminate, expunge the bloody incident from my life. How many synonyms are there for 'delete' in a thesaurus? Ask me. I know. I should know, for I have made a study of them in the seven years since the incident.

You'd think that as the days passed, things would get better... That it would get easier. That the horror of those hours when I had been forced to do things I'd never wish on another kid my age—or an adult, for that matter—would fade. Unfortunately, that isn't the case. It is the opposite, if that were possible. As if every minute that passes since the fateful day only cements the events that had taken place. That every hour that I've survived since, sharpens the focus on what happened. That every day I make it through, weighs me down, forces me to reconsider my options. That every month since, my resolve has only gotten stronger. I don't deserve to live. Not after what I did. Not after what was done to me. Not after what I was forced to feel, to sense, to experience...for I had been blindfolded for days. Then the blindfold was removed only to sear the events that took place into my memory via sight, before being replaced.

Throughout the incident I'd only been aware of one other person in the room, my friend Baron, who had been hauled into that space with me. We'd been separated from the five other boys who'd been kidnapped with us. Boys, I'd figured out, that I'd been acquainted with.

The seven of us had been from the same school. St. Lucian's. The school where the elite of the country send their spawn. Not ashamed to say, I was one of them. My parents had money. Lots of money. Money I hadn't cared about... Not until it had dawned on me that it was the reason I had landed up in that bullshit situation.

Kidnapped and held for ransom.

Kidnapped and...made to undergo things that should never be spoken of, or revealed. Kidnapped and helpless, blindfolded and bound, and hidden away for nearly a month, until we had been rescued. But by then, the damage had been done.

I'd been broken. Made to feel helpless, forced to surrender myself in the worst way possible. I'd had my heart, and my soul, and my very sense of being, ripped apart. Degraded and made to hate myself for how I had responded in those circumstances. It's why I hate myself. It's why… I must destroy myself.

Obliterate, demolish, raze to the ground... This self that feels like it no longer belongs to me.

I am floating, flying, running up the beach, faster, faster. Legs pumping, heels digging into the sand, kicking up fine particles in my wake. My heart pounds in my chest; the blood pumps in my veins. My pulse rate ratchets up as a gust of wind buffets me. I lean into it, tear through the breeze, push myself to speed up. Sweat beads my brow, slides down my temples. My shirt sticks to my back as I propel forward. Faster. Quicker. Reach for that which is not there. The emptiness, the vacant beyond. The horizon where the stars shine and beckon. The vast skies where I can float, merge, become one with the breeze. Scattered to the four corners.

Where there won't be any more use of this body. Where I won't need to live with the grief, the constant recriminations, the guilt, the questions that I pose to myself every bloody day. Where I don't need to face myself in the mirror. Where I won't see the features of every-thing I hate staring back at me day after day. Where I won't need… Anything. No more. Where I am no longer me.

No more Edward.

No more flinching away from the truth. No more trying to negate everything that has become of me. For there would only be a blank canvas… A life that has been reset. There would be no more need to carry the weight of this helplessness that clings to every pore of my body. This wondering if I could have done anything differently to prevent what had been done to me.

Why me? Why me? Why me? Why —

"Edward."

That isn't me. It can't be me.

"Ed!"

Leave me be. Please. Please. Please.

"Edward, you bastard!"

"What the —" My eyelids flutter open.

"You absolute, utter twat!"

I stare up into the burning blue gaze of my friend. My best friend, if you want to be technical, though I hate that phrase. We aren't teenaged girls, for hell's sake. We weren't even teenagers. Well, technically we are, for another year, considering we had both turned nineteen recently. And had celebrated with the rest of the Seven, in one hell of a piss up.

We'd gotten drunk and there had been pussy. A lot of pussy. We'd... All of us had indulged, gotten our dicks wet... Something which I had enjoyed more than I'd care to admit. The pleasures of the flesh are one way of shoving out all other thoughts from my head. It's either that or find oblivion in the sweet sting of the needle as it sinks into my blood stream. Something I've been turning to more and more often... Not ashamed to admit that. Why should I be, when it's the only thing that allows me to lurch from one stinking, hell-hole of a day to the next?

"You brain dead, shitstain," Baron growls. "The hell do you think you are doing?"

"What does it look like?" My voice seems to come from a distance.

"You're the arse end of a nuisance, you know that?"

"Takes one to know another." I smirk. Or at least, I think I do. I can't tell because my face is numb. Come to think of it, so are my fingers and my toes... Hell, most of my body. Whatever crazy shit I shot into myself has taken effect, which is good, right? I blink, try to push myself to sit up, only my body doesn't respond to my commands. Whoa. I try to raise my hand but my muscles don't move. Shit. Not good. Not good. All the nerve cells in my body light up. My brain cells —what's left of them, that is—ping a warning. *Get up, asshole. Scrape yourself off of the ground and try to stand up. Keep going; that's what you want, right? You do want that, don't you?*

"What the hell is wrong with you?"

2

Edward

Baron's jaw hardens. He grabs my shoulder, hauls me up. My head lolls. My back feels too disjointed to hold me up, and I slump back onto the floor.

"Shit. Shit. Shit." I hear Baron swearing above me as he grabs my shoulders and yanks me up to my feet. My knees buckle and I lean into him. He throws his arm around me, props me up. "What did you take, Ed?" he growls. "What have you shot yourself up with this time?"

"What the hell does it matter to you?"

"It shouldn't, you piece of crap," Baron snarls, "but unfortunately, I found you and if I let you die, I may never forgive myself."

"So, you're doing this for yourself?" I taunt.

"I'm doing this because you don't get to take the easy way out, you tosser."

"Trust me, nothing easy about it," I mutter.

"Trust me, from where I am, I am tempted to join you down there in your haze of forgetfulness."

"But you won't."

"Drugs are not my style," he declares as he begins to drag me toward the doorway of the room. "When I decide to go, it'll be in a blaze of glory."

"A-n-d, there you have it," I mutter to an imaginary audience, "the difference between this mofo here and me. I am willing to chase the high; you seek a high from the chase."

"What's the difference?" Baron scowls as he yanks me out of the room, down the steps, and away from the space where I'd hoped to end my life. Shit, one lousy thing I'd hope to accomplish and I've screwed that up too. I'd set myself one task. To shoot up enough that I wouldn't live to face the light again, and I hadn't managed to complete it. Why the hell am I so useless?

"The difference, Ed..." Baron's voice cuts through the thoughts rolling in my head.

"What?" I swallow, "What are you talking about?"

"The difference between chasing the high and seeking a high from the chase," he says patiently. "You were going to tell me the difference?"

What the hell is he talking about? Or is he talking just to keep me awake so I don't lapse into a sleep that I don't come back from? And would that be so bad?

He reaches the front door of the building, kicks it open, and yanks me out into the fresh air. Sunshine. Brightness. Argh. I throw up my arm… Or at least, I try to. Sadly, my body is still not responding to my instructions. What's the point of having arms and legs if they simply dangle at my sides, huh? Maybe if I simply stay still, try not to move, close my eyes and —

"Edward, wake the hell up."

Something connects with my cheek. The haziness in my head thins. I open my eyes to find I am on the sidewalk, on my back, Baron leaning over me.

"You slapped me, asshole?" I slur. "What the hell is wrong with you?"

"What's wrong with you?" he growls. "Why the hell are you trying to kill yourself."

"You know why," I mutter, "you were there too."

"That's the point, you douchebag." His jaw tics. "I was there too. I went through what you did too. I live through every harrowing second of those hours, but I am not here trying to shoot myself up with poison."

"No," I chuckle, "you're out chasing a different kind of high. The kind that comes with putting your life on the line with extreme sports."

"At least if I go, it will be mid-jump, or on my way to the bottom of the sea, or climbing a mountain. I'll be in full command of my senses and aware of what I am doing."

"You mean, unlike me?"

"You weren't like this Ed. You were never a coward."

"I'm not a hero either." My lips quirk. "I am not as strong as you, Baron."

"You're wrong. I am not bloody strong. I am broken inside, same as you Ed. I wake up every day, not sure if I can face the day. Not sure if I can look another person in the eye, and see the reflection of the horror that crawls inside of me. But I do it anyway."

"Well, good for you." I grimace. "Baron, the brave. Baron, the two-faced bastard who is so good at projecting a brave front to the world."

"If you think you can bait me, you're wrong." He grabs the front of my shirt, pulls me up to my feet. "If you think you can push me away, you're mistaken," he snaps.

I stumble then manage to find my balance. "What-bloody-ever." I smirk. The world spins around me and my knees buckle. He reaches for me and I lurch back.

"Leave, asshole," I mutter. "Why the hell are you here, in the first place? Didn't you get the memo? I am not interested in exchanging sob stories. I don't bloody care about what happened to you. I just want to be left alone, okay?"

I sway, try to brush past him, but he steps in my path.

"Where the hell are you going?"

"Inside." I take a sideways step and he mirrors my move. I scowl at him, "Get out of my way, you bastard."

"Not happening," he says in a calm voice. "If you think I'm going to let you go back in there and shoot up until you're dead, you have another think coming."

I sway, right myself. Focus on his face and his features split into two, then four. Oops. This can't be good. Or maybe it is. Maybe this is exactly how it should all go down.

"You're right." I smile. Darkness dots the edges of my vision. Sweat beads my brow and my shirt sticks to my back. I am burning up and cold. So cold. All at the same time. My thigh muscles spasm; my arms and legs tremble. I tuck my elbows close to my sides, draw myself up to my full height. "You're abso-bloody-right." I swallow.

"I am?" He scowls.

I nod. "I don't need to go back in there and shoot up until I am dead because I am on my way there now."

The blackness pulls me under.

I am floating…floating. I kick out, aim for the light that glimmers in the distance. If I can only make it there, I will be all right. If I reach that shining orb, things will sort themselves out. I will become whole again. I can fill this emptiness inside of me, rid myself of the anguish that festers inside of me. I can peel off the desolation that clings to me, and finally allow myself to be. I can rid myself of the story I have carried inside for so long, and revel in not being me.

I push forward, zero in on that luminescence. Closer, closer. The warmth intensifies as I get nearer. A sensation of being supported, held.

It's…a strange feeling to not be threatened. To be understood. To be allowed to experience every single emotion and none of it, at the same time. To not be judged. To be… Absolved of my guilt. My suffering. My misery. For the distress to fade away and be replaced by… Quiet. Peace. Living in the moment. Not yesterday, not tomorrow. Just the here and now. This, as I am, so it will be. This is me. This—suspended between death and life, between hell and heaven, between feeling too much and not feeling anything. This midway point is where everything begins and ends. This…is where I am supposed to be. This…is purity and profanity. Birth and leaving your body behind. This...is where you take your first breath. Your first step, that defines you all over again. This is where you start, for as you are, so you will be.

The light flickers, grows more distant. I pump my legs, shoot forward, but to no avail. The separation increases and I know I want to get closer. Feel those few seconds of how it had been to be one with myself. With the presence that had filled me, engulfed me, shown me the way. If I can only experience that moment of completeness again… One more time. Just one more time. That's all I seek.

I reach out with my hand, and someone grasps it. I try to open my eyes, blink, and shut them again.

"He's awake."

There's movement above me, and someone speaking. The words fade in and out of my consciousness. Bright light overwhelms me.

When I open my eyes again, it's to face those same cold blue ones. "You?" I groan, "Why the hell can't I get rid of you?"

"The bastard saved your life. You could try to be a bit more grateful," a familiar voice drawls.

I turn my head, groan when I take in the man on the couch in the far corner of the room. Next to him, Saint glowers at me. Arpad, Damian and Weston, the rest of the Seven are sprawled around the space. All of them meet my gaze with varying expressions of hurt and anger. So much anger. Shit, they are not going to let this pass.

"Have I died and gone to hell?" I finally venture.

"You wish," Sinclair drawls as he leans forward, "that would have made things so much easier."

"Unfortunately for us, you are very much alive, pisstard," Saint growls.

"What the hell were you thinking?" Damian demands. "Shooting yourself up with enough substances to floor an elephant? Seriously,

Ed?" He slams his fist into the palm of his hand, "What the hell is wrong with you?"

"He's a bloody coward, that's what he is." Arpad growls. "Asshole, wants to take the easy way out."

"Is that right?" Saint scowls. "You want to check out, is that right, Ed? You want to give up and stop fighting? You think you are the only one in pain, asshole? Well, you are wrong." Saint gets to his feet and stalks over to me. "You think Baron, here, has had it easier? You think any of us here have managed to have a normal life after the bloody incident?"

I hold his gaze, take in his flushed features. "I, uh, didn't expect any of you guys to take it this personally."

"Take it personally?" Arpad mutters. "Of course, we take it personally. You are one of us, bro. One of the Seven, bound by an event that turned all of our lives upside down. We are, each of us, struggling to come to grips with it in, our own way. Admittedly, we all have our own ways of coping with it," he raises his shoulders, "and sometimes, it gets to be too much. I get it." He drums his fingers on his thigh, "I get that it can get overwhelming and sometimes, you need to get it out of your system —"

"Which is why we have the underground fights," Sinclair murmurs, "so we can beat the shit out of those foolish enough to volunteer for fights —"

"Or each other." Saint smirks.

"Failing which, you can always talk it out," Weston offers. "You could get help —"

"No," I swallow, "no therapy."

"What then?" Baron barks. "You continue to shoot yourself up the first chance you get, until you OD and die? Is that your big plan?"

"Yes," I turn to him, "that had been my plan."

"Had been." He scowls, "So, it's not so any longer?"

"Let's just say, I have no wish to repeat this experience again."

He snorts, "You expect me to believe that?"

"Believe it…or not." I raise a shoulder, "All I can tell you is that I am not going to try that stunt again."

"To what do we owe this sudden resolve?" Sinclair drawls. "Don't tell me you saw the light when you almost died?"

There's silence in the room. For a beat, another, then Baron swears, "Shit." He rubs his chin, "You actually did have some kind of realization or something."

"Or something," I agree. "It was…" I glance around the room, "It was a moment of clarity… No, not even that. It was," I search for the words, "a few seconds of just being. Know what I mean?"

The men shake their heads. I turn to Baron, who's watching me carefully, "Don't tell me you saw God?" His tone is light, but his voice is wary.

"I saw… No… I felt… Like I was in the presence of something that was definitely like nothing I have felt before," I finally say.

"Hmm." He folds his arms over his chest, "I'm all for it, if it means that it keeps you out of drug dens."

"It will," I reply. "I am not going back there again."

"And you are going to get yourself cleaned up?" He scowls. "You're going to get into rehab and rid yourself of that nasty habit?"

"Do I have a choice?"

"Nope," he growls. "Where do you think you are now? Already checked you in, as a matter of fact, and the bill's all paid up. With your money."

"My money?"

"Your parents footed the bill."

"Of course, they did," I murmur. "Anything to get their errant spawn off their backs."

They haven't come to visit, though. Clearly, they can't bear to ruin their public image by acknowledging that their only son is a junkie.

"Who cares whether your family likes you or not?" Weston scowls. "As long as the Seven of us stick together, we should be fine."

"You're one to talk. You and bastard Beauchamp, here," Damian jerks his chin toward Arpad, "have the most supportive families amongst us. Not that I am complaining," he adds. "The less you have to do with blood family, the less therapy you need for the damage they inflict on you."

"Jeez, that's cynical, don't you think?" Arpad frowns. "Okay, so I know I have a more understanding family, as compared to most of you, but still." He shakes his head, "Family is important. Both made family," he gestures to us, "and the blood one."

"Can't speak to the latter, ol' chap." Sinclair rises to his feet, "And that, I believe, is my cue to get the fuck out of here and get working on the algorithm."

"Algorithm?"

"Yeah," Saint unfolds his frame from the couch, "Sinner and I have been working on one to crack the stock market patterns. We believe we should be able to create an algo which predicts trends on the stock market."

"That's bloody impressive." I jerk my chin, "And quite a feat, if you do achieve it."

"Oh, we will," Sinner smirks, "and when we do, it's going to catapult us straight into the ranks of the richest in the country."

Money. It's important. It's also what landed all of us in this mess of a situation. You want it, but also don't want too much of it to screw up your life. And shit... That encounter with whatever-it-was, when I was knocked out, has clearly, rewired my brain in some way. I've always been introspective, but now, it feels like I am on the verge of some kind of breakthrough.

The rest of the men rise to their feet.

"We should be off then." Saint walks over and we bump fists. The rest of the guys follow in variations of the same as they bid goodbye. They trickle out until it's only Baron and me in the room.

"I'd best get going too." He pushes up from the chair and turns to go.

"Baron," I call out, "thank you."

He pauses and turns to stare at me over his shoulder. "Don't thank me," he growls, "just stay out of your own head for a while, will you?"

"If only it were that easy."

"It's only as difficult as you make it out to be."

"You wanted to know the difference between chasing the high and seeking a high from the chase."

He scowls. "What is it?"

"The former is me, of course. Or, it *was* me." I lower my chin. "The latter…is you —finding new ways to put your life on the line, and each time you walk away unscathed, wondering why you're still alive."

"Is that your observation?"

"It's my conclusion."

"You're wrong."

"I am?"

"Each time I skydive, I know the risks I am taking. I have carefully trained for it. In fact," he widens his stance, "there's a 99.99% chance of surviving a skydive."

"What about the 0.0007% chance of dying?"

"That?" His grin broadens, "That's where the fun starts."

3

Baron

I inspect the three-ring release system on the container holding my parachute to be sure it's clear. Make sure the straps across my chest and my two leg straps are routed through their buckles.

Then check the three handles on my straps.

Check my shoes, helmet, altimeter, goggles.

This is my third check. One check, I'd conducted after I'd put on the gear. The next, after getting on the flight. The third is now, just before I jump. That doesn't even count my initial visual inspection when I picked up my gear.

I hadn't been lying when I'd told Edward that I go into all of my skydives well prepared. There's a difference between taking a carefully calculated risk versus thrill-seeking. And while I wish I could end my life every day, it's precisely that which makes me doubly careful when I prepare for a jump. It's almost like, every time I jump, I am daring the elements to push me over the edge, against all odds. To jump out of the plane and land on the surface unscathed. Each time I do so, I know I am using up a life. How many lives will it take for my time here to run out?

I have no illusions about that. I know my time here is short. I have no wish to prolong it. Yet, I also seek a reason to live, something I don't have yet.

Edward had reacted to the incident by looking inside himself, by retreating on journeys through his inner space, trying to figure out what it is that holds him connected to himself.

Me? I've gone the other way. Pushing myself beyond my boundaries, stepping out of my comfort zone, taking chances with myself in the hope of finding out why it is that I had survived the incident. Why am I still alive? What do I hope to accomplish by having made it this far? As I complete my checks and stand poised by the door of the plane, I can see my past rush before my eyes.

Each time I jump, every single moment of my life—the good, the bad…and especially, every single second of those wretched days when I had been held captive, when I had been made to do things against my will that nobody living should ever have to do—all of that, flashes before of my eyes. It happens so quickly, my mind hasn't the bandwidth to assimilate what I'm seeing. It's happening to someone else. Then all thoughts fade away.

The door opens, a sudden rush of cold wind slams into me and goosebumps rise on my skin. I look down and see the ground thousands of feet below. My heart begins to race and the pulse pounds at my temples. Adrenaline laces my blood and I jump. I flatten my elbows against my body, thrust my chin forward as I go into free fall. The wind rushes over me as my heartbeat ratchets up. Then a calm fills me. The sound of the wind fills my ears, the space between my ears pushing everything else out. I free fall, and fall, and fall, and continue to fall.

I pull the ripcord, glance up, find the parachute hasn't deployed yet.

I stare down at the ground rushing up to meet me. I can make out the roads cutting through the fields, the vehicles moving along it, the green stretching out in between. Sunshine dapples off the blue of the river that snakes across the landscape, intersecting with one of the roads before it continues its journey to the sea. What is my destination? Have I come this far, only to die, splattered across a shit-stained country farm somewhere?

It would serve me right if I do. I don't deserve better. I had been in that situation and had allowed myself to be manipulated. I had allowed myself to be threatened. I had given in to the fear then. I will not give into it now. I will face my death head on. This…this is why I have been skydiving. I've pretended it was for the excitement, for the control. Knowing that I held my life in my own hands every time I jumped out of a plane…

But I had been wrong. I had been tempting death each time. Knowing if I dived enough times, the odds would catch up with me. Being extra careful with my gear as a way to taunt death. To show that I wasn't going to give in that easily. And here I am, facing the inevitable.

My throat dries. The pressure builds behind my eyes. Tears blur my line of sight… And it has to be because of the breeze hitting my face, right? I stare down at the ground, so much closer now. I can make out the details of the fields, the yellows and the light greens, the brown indicating a recent harvest…or a space yet to be seeded for the next crop.

Will I live long enough to see another season, another day… Another life? Do I want to live another life when I haven't even managed to figure this one out? Do I want to die? Am I ready to die? To leave behind my friends, and a future I haven't even begun to embrace? Do I want to run away, let the fear overwhelm me?

Will I allow the remorse over what had happened to get the better of me?

Allow the hate at what had happened to overpower me? Consume me, bring me to my knees?

Am I going to give up without even having tried to own my destiny?

And after criticizing Ed for trying to take the easy way out...

Fucking fuck. I take in the details of the farm I had spotted earlier. The neat buildings, the sheds, the tractor plowing the field, the truck that stands in the driveway. Then I reach up, use the handle to cut away the main parachute. Tug on the second handle to release the reserve, and it inflates. Instantly, I stop falling.

The wind drops in force and I float. Float. I can hear my heart beat in my ears. Feel the pulse in my throat. My fingers tingle, my limbs tremble. I draw in a breath, another, focus on taking in the wide expanse of the blue sky, the vastness and me but a dot in time; knowing it will be over all too soon and wanting to prolong this moment when it feels like I am flying. I am free. Not bound by my past. Not tied down to the future. Just now. Just here. Now. Me. I glance down to find my feet approach the ground. My feet graze the mud. I stumble forward land on my knees then roll over onto the muddy field.

The parachute lines tug on me as they hit the ground behind me. I lay there, winded, gazing at the blue sky above. Puffs of clouds float by. A light wind ruffles the canopy of the parachute. Sunshine warms my face, and I lift my chin. I am alive. Guess I really didn't want to die.

I'd flirted with the idea, had come so close to letting go. All I'd had to do…was nothing. Not pull the handle of the reserve parachute and I'd have smashed into the ground. It would all have been over so easily. So quickly. I'd never have to face another flashback to the incident. Never have to wake up at night, sweating and unable to breathe. Never have to drag myself out of bed in the morning, wondering how I am going to get through the day.

I've never revealed to the Seven just how much the incident haunts my nights and every waking moment… Not even to Edward, who knows exactly what went down that day. Unlike him, I'm not able to vent the distress that I carry around inside—the guilt, the self-reproach of what I had had to do that day. The shame. Even as the logical part of me protests that I wasn't responsible for what happened. It's not my fault that I was kidnapped or made to take part in those heinous activities…

Yet something else inside of me, insists that it was me. I did something to make myself stand out, to be marked for the kidnapping. I caught their eye. I'm the reason we were separated from the other boys… For what I had then been able to do.

Fuck. I squeeze my fingers at my sides. On second thought, maybe I should have simply not pulled that reserve parachute. I should have crashed to the ground, allowed the blackness of possible death to engulf me. I'd had the chance and I'd let it go... Because... I'm not ready. Not to die. Not to give up. Not to roll over and live life traumatized by my past.

I'd had a chance to break free, to cut the cord that connects me to the weight of the wrong that had been done to me. And while I may never outrun the nightmares, I can make sure that my days are focused on becoming a better version of myself.

A face looms over me, cutting off the sight of the blue skies.

"You okay, man?" a guy asks.

I blink, take in his features. The hair cut close to his scalp. He's young, close to my age, probably, and wearing military fatigues.

"Need help?" He extends his arm. I grab his hand and he hauls me to my feet.

The weight of the parachute pulls at me and I stagger. I slough off the parachute that I had so carefully snapped on not too long ago. Then rise to my full height.

The stranger jerks his chin toward the remnants of the canopy, "Need help with that?"

Together, we roll up the parachute, then haul it to the side of a nearby barn.

"I'm Archer, by the way," He straightens, holds out his palm, "Archer Feldman."

"Baron," I reply, "Baron Masters."

"You do this often?" He gestures to the parachute, "Skydiving?"

"That was my one-hundredth jump."

"One-hundredth?" He frowns. "How long have you been jumping out of planes?"

"Long enough to have a healthy respect for the fact that I survived that fall."

"Your parachute didn't deploy?" He glances at my rolled up parachute, "And the reserve didn't open quickly enough?"

I hesitate, then tilt my head, "Opened quickly enough for me to land without any injury."

"You were lucky."

Was I? "Or in the right place at the right time." *Unlike the incident.* All it takes is a hair's breadth of an alteration and things can change, as I'd just demonstrated. If I hadn't pulled the handle of the reserve parachute, things would have looked very different about now. But I had, and I had made the choice to move forward. "And you?" I look him up and down, "You're in the army?"

"I just got back from deployment a few hours ago."

"And all this?" I glance around the space, "This is yours?"

"Belonged to my parents," he shuffles his feet, "who are no more."

"I'm sorry for your loss."

He inclines his head. "It was a couple of years ago, just after I turned eighteen. I've managed this place with the help of a caretaker since. And you?" He scrutinizes my features, "What do you do, when you are not falling out of planes?"

"That's the question, isn't it?" I rub the back of my neck. "I'm trying to figure out where I am headed next."

He watches me closely, then nods, "Want to come in and get cleaned up, get a bite to eat, meanwhile?"

4

———————

Baron

I face off against Arpad in the underground parking lot on the
outskirts of London. What had started months ago as a means for the
seven of us to let off steam has snowballed into a crowd puller.

Guys—and girls—turn up every week to watch us, knowing they
are guaranteed a good fight. One of us going up against the other,
until someone is knocked out cold. Or close to it.

After I'd accepted Archer's invitation to lunch, we'd chatted.
Turns out, he'd enrolled in the Army a year ago, at nineteen, had been
deployed to Afghanistan. He'd returned from his first tour and
couldn't wait to get back. The excitement in his voice, the zeal, the
focus, his pride in being part of something larger than himself... All of
it had come as a breath of fresh air. I'd left, convinced that this was
the route forward for me.

To channel my angst, my hatred, my anger at what happened to
me into something that would serve my country and benefit so many

others. Also, the challenge of pitting myself against the rigors of making it through the recruitment process. More than half of the applicants either drop out or get dropped, or so Archer had told me. He'd asked me if I was up to the challenge? And of course, I'd decided right then, that if I do decide to enlist, no way am I not making it through the recruitment phase with anything less than flying colors.

By the time my ride arrives, I am convinced that this is my future. I haven't mentioned anything to the Seven, though. Not even to Edward. It's not like this is a secret, just... I prefer to keep my cards close to my chest. The rest of the Seven all but live in each other's pockets, the way they hang out with each other. Me? I prefer to keep to myself. Not that I have anything against any of them. Hell, I owe it to them that I made it through the days following the incident.

My family had grappled with it, tried to work out how they were going to deal with a son who was so clearly traumatized. Their answer? To throw money at it. I'd received the best therapy, the best help possible... Everything, except my own parents spending time with me. My sister had wanted to help, but they'd decided they didn't want me to corrupt her with my presence. As if just being with me would result in something similar happening to her. So, they'd shipped her off to boarding school, and they'd have done the same to me, except my therapist made it clear that it wouldn't help me at all to have so much change thrust on me while already being a fragile state.

So, they'd let me be; let me exist in that massive home of theirs. A place I hate almost as much as I've begun to loathe them. It's another reason shipping off to the army makes so much sense. I won't have to see them for a long time again. Not until the time comes for me to access my trust fund, and if I'm lucky, not even then. It's money my grandfather left me and which I will be able to access when I turned twenty-one. Money I can use in whatever way I see fit. Money which will make me completely independent.

Money which I will inherit, provided I make it through this round with the asshole I am taking on. I throw up my fists, circle Arpad. Around us, money exchanges hands as the spectators bet on either of us. Not that the Seven have any lack of access to funds, considering the billions that their families share between them. It's the principle of the thing, though. They want to watch us fight, they have to pay. And the people are more than happy to do that. After all, the privilege of seeing one rich brat kick the shit out of the other is more entertaining than reality TV, which is what they'd be binging on instead, if they didn't have this.

I move slowly, lock my gaze with Arpad as I circle. Draw in a breath, as I bide my time. Wait. Wait. Arpad scowls; sweat beads his forehead. His shoulders bunch and his biceps twitch. Asshole can't wait to fight. He's quick to the draw, impatient. Me? I am happy to draw him out. To extend this encounter for as long as it takes. That's my strength; I have infinite patience. I can wait for the other man to make a mistake, before I make my move. All I have to do is bide my time. So, I force myself to relax, empty my mind of all thoughts except the focus in my opponent's gaze. His nostrils flare and the tendons of his throat move as he swallows. His gaze narrows and the hair on the nape of my neck rises.

I sense his intent to attack a few seconds before he charges me. I swoop to the side, pivot, throw my arm around his neck, and yank. The force of it has us pitching backward. I release him, hit the ground and roll to the side, just as he hits the ground where I'd been. The vibrations from the fall travel through me as I push up, turn, and straddle my fallen friend. I bury my fist in the side of his face and blood gushes from his mouth. I pull back, land another to his shoulder, to his side, back to his face. He blocks me, with his left arm, grabs my shoulder with his other, shoves me back with enough force that I lose my balance.

Instantly, he's on me. He flings me off. I hit the ground on my back, and it's his turn to straddle me, to land a fist in my shoulder, then swipe one in the direction of my face. I block him, hit out and get him with an uppercut.

The force of my hit throws him off. He lands on his back only to spring up to his feet at the same time as me. This time we both rush at each other. Our chests collide as we wrap our arms around one another, fighting for good arm and hip position. My chest heaves and my entire body hurts from the beating I have taken so far, but I don't give up. I dig my heels into the ground as we both jostle for a chance to take the other down. I rear back, head butt him in the cheek.

Arpad growls as blood rains down his face. I pull back, bring up my knee to his mid-section. He grunts as the air whooshes out of him. He stumbles and I step back, only to reach down, grab one of his legs, lift it off the ground and topple him.

He hits the ground with a thud, only to scissor his legs and grab me around the waist. We grapple in that position for a few seconds. Then I lunge my upper body forward. Slide my legs apart for leverage. Grab his face between my forearms as I bracket his neck between my elbows and begin to choke him. He gasps, tries to draw in a breath, fails, and his entire body shudders.

"Give up," I growl, "I've won this."

He shakes his head, and I lean my entire body weight into the position. His face grows purple and the veins at his temple bulge. Then he taps my arm. I loosen my grip and he lets go of me. I straighten, shake my head, turn to the stunned audience.

I raise my arms, throw my head back and yell. And it's like a signal to the rest. The crowd roars; men raise their fists. A few girls surge forward, only to be stopped by the rest of the Seven, who have positioned themselves at strategic positions around the perimeter of the makeshift circle that forms the fighting ring.

Sweat drips off of my face as I take in the crowd of faces. Most are screaming, hanging onto the temporary barriers that cordon off the fighting ring. I spot one guy staring at us. He's our age, tall and skinny, with gaunt features and dark circles under his eyes. He looks familiar. Where have I seen him before?

He's wearing jeans and a hoodie covers his hair. His gaze bores into me. He stares at me, then at Arpad on the ground. Takes in the rest of the Seven before his gaze darts back to me.

Something about his features, the way he stands... I am not sure what, but my hackles rise. I take a step toward him and he stiffens. He steps back and is swallowed up by the rest of the crowd. *Huh. What was that about?*

Then I see Sinner walking toward us as Arpad staggers to his feet.

He grabs our wrists, glares around the crowd for a second, then raises my arm. "We have a fucking winner," he shouts. "Take your winnings, or forever hold your piss."

5

Baron

Twenty minutes later, I glance up from the chair I am sprawled in. We are in the trailer that is parked at the edge of the parking lot. It's also our unofficial green room, of sorts. And not only because it's moldy... it's here where we count our winnings. Har, har. Poor joke. You're welcome, by the way.

Weston has bandaged my wounds, which aren't that many. Unlike Arpad, whose face is a bloody mess. A bandage covers his left cheek, where I'd sunk my fist.

"You look none the worse for the wear, ol' chap," I smirk.

"And you look," he glares at me, "too bloody smug."

"Hey, I won fair and square." My grin widens. "Admit it. I am a better fighter than you."

"You got lucky this time," he grumbles. "I'll get you in the next fight."

"Keep dreaming." I glance up as the other boys troop in.

"That was a bloody good fight." Saint bounces into the room, "Of course, if I'd been fighting, I would've felled Arpad in half the time."

"No, you wouldn't've." Arpad scowls. "I'm a better fighter than you."

"Want me to prove it to you?" Saint throws up his fists as Edward ambles in.

He brushes past Saint, to throw himself onto the hammock that's strung up in a corner of the space. "I'm hungry," he mutters. "All that fighting... It's given me a hell of an appetite."

"Me too," Damian groans from the armchair he occupies in the corner. His long hair flows about his shoulders, his eyelids at half-mast as he stares down at the woman who kneels between his legs. He looks every inch like the rockstar in training that he is. He folds his arms behind his neck, yawns. Yep, right down to that jaded act that he portrays so well, and at the tender age of nineteen. "Nothing like a good fight to get the juices flowing." He smirks.

No kidding. "Arpad and I are the ones who fought, you dip shit. By rights, we should be the only ones who are hungry."

"Hey, come on, we're growing boys." Saint protests, "We need our sustenance, and not only in the form of pussy." He lowers his gaze to the girl in front of Damian, who leans in and begins to move up and down, clearly putting herself into the task on hand.

"You have ten seconds to get me off," Damian informs her. "That is, if you want another chance at worshipping at the altar of future greatness."

"Worshipping at the altar of...?" I scowl. "Who do you think you are? The next Led Zeppelin?"

"Better," he bares his teeth, "I'll be the one and only Damian Savage to have graced the annals of rock history."

The girl's shoulders snap back, her breathing audible in the room.

Damian sighs, then pats her head. "You may leave now."

She leans back, wipes her hand across her lips, "B...but..."

"That was excellent for a one-off," he informs her, "but my friends are waiting, and bros before hos, and all that."

He jerks his chin, and she rises to her feet.

"You...you'll call when you feel the need?"

"No promises, babe. You knew what you were getting into when you volunteered your services in the first place."

"Can I at least get a selfie?" she whines

"You know the rules; no pictures allowed in here." He raises a finger and points it to the door, "Off you go, now."

She looks like she is about to protest, then pivots and marches to the door.

"Since when did we decide no pictures in the dressing room?" I scowl as the door snicks shut behind her.

"Since I've had a stalker showing up on my social media sites making threats."

"Bro, you've arrived." Saint shakes his head, "To think, people actually pay to hear you yowl."

"Most likely, it's some girl you treated like shit," I mutter.

Saint snorts.

Damian glowers.

"I'll make you yowl, you mofo." Damian closes his pants. He springs up, heads in Saint's direction, when Sinner steps between them.

"Let's cut the shit and get out of here." He holds up a paper envelope, then glances around the room. "These here are the winnings from the fine fight that you gentleman put up today. What say we go and blow some of this on a slap-up meal?"

The next day we meet at lunch time at one of our favorite pubs. It's on the outskirts of the city, not far from Saint's uncle's urban farm, where we had stopped off first to help out with the horses. The pub itself is buzzing, this time of the day. Like many British pubs, this one has transformed itself into a bit of a gastro-pub, complete with a chef who cooks really well. It attracts both noobs like me and the Seven, as well as families who stop off the highway, in search of a decent meal.

I pile my plate with fried chicken, mashed potatoes, a well-done burger, and waffles on top, because, yeah, I'm not hungry at all. My stomach rumbles, and I pick up my knife and fork. I tear into the waffle, while Edward eyes my portions. "I don't think you have enough on that plate."

"Hmm." I chew on my food, swallow it, then glance around the table. Stick my fork into a potato and place it on top of the pile. "There, that's better, isn't it?"

Edward grimaces, turns back to his plate. I take in the roast duck on his plate. "That's all you are having?"

"Nope." He cuts into his food, swallows a mouthful, "I am just not eating everything, all at the same time."

I stare down at my plate, then at his again, "You may have a point… Not." I smirk, "Why wait, when you can have everything at the same time?"

"Why try to sample everything all at once, when you can take your time and savor the taste of each mouthful?"

"And there you have it, ladies," Saint drawls, "the difference between the two of you."

"Which is?" I scowl.

"Yeah, enlighten us, oh wise soul," Edward scoffs.

"Speaks for itself, doesn't it?" He glances at my plate, "Our man Baron, here, clearly, prefers to cram as much as he can into the moment. While Ed—" He turns to Edward's plate, "He errs on the side of caution. Likes to take his time to savor what he has." He stares between us, "In a sense, you guys are two sides of the same coin."

"How so?" I frown.

"You make sure you never lose an opportunity; you make the most of everything you can get your hands on in the moment, while, Ed," he jerks his chin in Ed's direction, "he relishes whatever is in front of him. So, both of you, in a sense, want to live in the present. You both want to take hold of everything in front of you and make sure you indulge yourself. You both want to let go of the past; you both don't want to worry about the future. Ergo, you like to be in the moment… Which is the toughest thing anyone can do, and yet, both of you make it look so easy." He laughs. "Not." Saint lays down his fork, "Any of you guys fancy another round of beer?"

At our nods, he gets up from the table, stalks off to the bar to order.

This pub is an original, meaning, you need to order food and drinks at the bar and they bring it to you. Also, families, including dogs, are welcome.

A peal of laughter breaks through my thoughts. I turn, and in the adjoining dining room, I see a girl who must be nine or ten, talking animatedly to her sister. She's wearing a red dress. The sunshine slants in through the window and highlights her auburn locks. The red highlights glint, and for a second, it's as if there's a halo around her head.

She laughs again, and the sound is so musical, so carefree... When is the last time I felt that way? Just living in the moment, without being burdened by my past. Without the constant ache that I seem to carry inside me. I'd do anything to feel so free, so innocent again.

Saint walks back, with a pitcher and I turn back to the boys, follow along with their half-assed jokes. I glance down at my heaped plate but don't feel like eating anymore. I reach for my pint of beer, down half of it, then wipe the foam off my upper lip as I glance sideways at the table again. Only the space is empty.

Huh, did I imagine it? Was the girl actually there? And why the hell am I so curious about her? She was only a kid... And yet, something about how she'd laughed and tossed her head of curls, it hinted at the woman she'll become one day, which... Is none of my business. I don't know her at all. Probably won't ever see her again.

"Baron." There's a touch on my shoulder. I turn to find Damian staring at me. "You okay, man?" he asks.

I nod.

"You look pale," he comments.

"Only because I have been spending too much time in the presence of you reprobates." I grimace.

Damian smirks, "Let's get out of here."

6

Six months later

Edward

"What the bloody hell—?" I watch as Baron launches across the short space that constitutes the fighting ring of the street-fight organized by the Bratva.

We are in the warehouse where the Kings of the Alley street fight organized by the Bratva takes place every week. Dumbass Damian had made a deal with them. The Bratva would get him onto one of the most prestigious venues in London to perform his first gig. In return, Damian would take on their best fighter, aka the Incredible Hulk—only uglier—a guy who shakes off Baron like he's the Ant Man.

Yeah, Baron had taken Damian's place because he is a better fighter, but clearly, he is no match for the Russian street fighter who heads toward his prone body. I move forward, pause when Baron jumps to his feet. The two circle each other.

The crowd begins to chant...

"Go Dima."
"Dima."
"Dima."

Obviously, they support Baron's opponent. Not a surprise, given this is the Russians' home ground. Dima lowers his head and charges toward Baron, who tries to sidestep but is not fast enough. His adversary smashes into Baron and the two go down.

Shit. I race toward the man guarding the gate to the makeshift ring, Saint and Arpad at my heels. The guard throws a punch. I duck, rush in. Behind me, I hear the sounds of a scuffle, while Arpad charges past me. He grasps Dima's shoulders, shoves him off of Baron. I reach Baron, Saint right behind me. We haul him up to his feet, drag him out of the makeshift arena. I turn, glance back to find Arpad getting in a direct hit to Dima's head, then his chest...to the stomach, to the side, the chest— I straighten, and with Saint's help, drag Baron through the crowd. We haul him toward the cordoned-off space at the side that passes for a dressing room. We half-carry, half-drag him inside and pour him into the lone chair.

I lean back, chest heaving. "You're bloody heavy, you know that?" I grouse.

Baron shakes his head, blood pouring from a cut in his lip. "Why the fuck did you drag me from there?" He lurches to his feet, takes a step forward and pales. "Shit." He grimaces. "The asshole broke my ankle." He sways, then sinks back into the chair.

"Erm," I glower, "do you want to ask that question again?"

"We saved your sorry arse from being ground into the dust, bitch," Saint snarls. "What the fuck is wrong with you, volunteering to take him on in the first place?"

"Why didn't you let Arpad take on the challenge to begin with?" I scowl at the wanker. "He's bigger than you, better suited in size to take on Incredible Hulk, out there."

Baron growls again. "I could do it..." He bunches his fingers into fists, "I can still defeat him." He squares his shoulders, "Just need to get back in the ring." He rises to his feet, sways, but stays standing.

Saint and I exchange glances. Then Saint taps him on the shoulder, and he collapses back into the chair.

"You were saying?" Saint smirks. Baron scowls.

I glower back at him. "Let Arpad finish him off, you ass. Sit this one out, will you?"

"No," he snaps.

"Yes," I insist, "you don't have to fight every battle that comes your way."

We scowl at each other and Saint throws up his hands. "You two... Why the hell do you always end up locking horns?" He stares at me, "You got this? Because much as I like to hang out with you two idiots... Not." He grimaces. "I'd better head out and see how things are out there."

Without waiting for a reply, he pivots and heads out of the cordoned off space. Baron and I glower at each other.

"The fuck is wrong with you?" I lean forward on the balls of my feet. "You could have gotten seriously injured, thanks to that stupid pride of yours."

"Yeah," he mutters, "but I can't back down from a challenge, you know that."

"Is that why you're still taking part in your extreme sports?"

"Among other things."

"What's that supposed to mean?" I frown

"Nothing." He mumbles. Footsteps sound, then Weston walks in. He places the first-aid kit on the floor next to Baron, pulls out what he needs, and proceeds to clean the wound on his lip.

Baron grimaces. "Shit, that hurts."

"Good." Weston scowls at him. "That was a stupid move, insisting on being in the ring with a man almost twice your size."

"It's good practice," he mutters.

"Practice?" I tilt my head, "For what?"

Before Baron can respond, Weston applies butterfly bandages to the wound on his lip. Baron closes his eyes, leans back in the stool. Weston takes care of the cut on his cheekbone, then bends to examine Baron's ankle. "It's not broken," Weston murmurs, "but you need to keep it elevated for a few days, keep the weight off."

Baron doesn't reply.

Weston straightens, turns to me. "You guys okay?"

Neither of us speak.

Weston packs up his first aid kit, then straightens, "You know, the only way to clear whatever grudge it is the two of you have with each other is to talk about it."

Baron snorts.

I raise a shoulder. If only it were that easy. The stuff that Baron and I went through... No kid should ever have to experience anything like that. No adult either. But we did. And now we are are... Fuck, if everything isn't a bloody disaster.

Weston scowls at each of us. "If I leave, you won't attack each other or something, will you?"

"Don't worry, Mom," Baron drawls, "your wards are not going to kill themselves when they are not on your watch."

Weston chuckles, "If you want me to leave so you guys can have a tete-a-tete, then you only needed to tell me."

"Just get out of here, will ya?" I mutter.

Weston snatches up the first kit and marches out, leaving the two of us in silence. Neither of us breaks it. For a beat, another.

Finally, Baron, pops open one swollen eyelid, "You're really doing it, aren't you?" he demands. "You're joining the bloody seminary."

"I am," I say in an even tone.

"Awesome." He straightens to his feet, winces, but stays standing. "Good luck with that, and whatever else you decide to do with your life." He limps past me, his shoulder bumps mine as he heads towards the perimeter of the space.

"Wait," I frown, "what did you mean by that?"

"By what?"

"By whatever bullshit it is you just said?"

He clicks his tongue, "No swearing; remember, you're going to become a priest?"

"Fuck that." I clench my fists at my sides, "What the hell are you going to do, Baron?"

"Wrong question." He smirks at me over his shoulder. "You should have asked me where I am headed."

"Where are you headed?"

"Somewhere far away from you lot, hopefully."

My heart thuds in my chest. *Shit, shit, shit.* "What the hell does that mean?"

He yawns, "Seriously, Ed, you're beginning to resemble a nagging old lady."

"And you..." I grit my teeth, "you're like an errant child who doesn't know his arse end from his front."

"Temper, temper." His grin widens, "You've made up your mind on what you want to do with your life, and now it's my turn."

He turns, walks away, and I spring into action. I jump toward him, grab him by his shoulder and yank him around. "What the bloody hell?" I shout. "What the fuck are you going to do, you bastard?"

He winces, glances down at where I am gripping his shoulder. "Let go of me," he says in a hard voice.

I hesitate, and he snaps, "I mean it, Ed."

"First, tell me what the hell you are going to do?"

"First, let go off me."

We glare at each other, then I release him. "There," I mutter, "now tell me what you are up to."

"Wouldn't you like to know?" Turning, he hobbles out of the area.

What in the everlovin'—? Stunned, I watch him for a few seconds before I give chase. I run after him, but despite his impeded gait, he's already managed to cut through a part of the crowd and is half-way to the exit. I pause near where the rest of the Seven are huddled,

"Baron, you fucker. Where the hell do you think you're going?"

My voice rings out above the noise of the crowd. From the corner of my eye, I notice Sinner and the rest of the guys glancing between us.

Baron reaches the exit, pauses, then turns. He seems to take in the scene, glances at each of the Seven in turn before his gaze settles on me. He jerks his chin, or at least, I think that's what he does. Then turning, he stalks out.

7

____

Eight years later

Baron

"Heathrow Express departs from platform two in ten minutes. Will passengers please make their way to…"

I tune out the rest of the announcement from the overhead speakers in the station. That's my train. It'll take me to Heathrow airport to catch a flight to Spain. It's where I've set up home, temporarily, since being discharged from the army.

I'd flown to London for forty-eight hours to catch up with my team of investigators who kept me informed about the movements of the Seven. Not that I don't trust the Seven… After all, they've kept me appraised of how my shares are doing. They've also informed me of all major decisions taken. It's just, I prefer to have first-hand intel of what they are up to. Our friendships aside, ultimately, we are also rivals, and the best way to protect my assets is to ensure I have knowledge of their dealings.

Still, I have to admit that most of their business recommendations over the past years have only helped to multiply the value of my stock. Basically, I am a billionaire without having to be actively involved in the running of the business. Something which suits me fine, right now.

Seven years ago, I walked out of the Kings of the Alley showdown and joined the army. Nineteen years old. Meeting Archer had been pivotal in my decision. He had offered me a way out of the situation I had found myself in. Emotionally trapped in my head, unable to move beyond the throes of the nightmare the incident had been, I'd been on a downward spiral, risking my life with my need for speed, addicted to the rush of adrenaline that laced my blood with every skydiving jump I'd taken. And it hadn't stopped there. I'd embarked on sampling every possible adventure sport that I came across. Cliff diving, BASE jumping, rock climbing, even shark diving...

The last... Okay, I hadn't enjoyed it much. Turns out, I prefer it when I'm not in a cage...on the ocean floor...surrounded by sharks. Kind of makes me feel like I'm not in control. I'd much rather be on the outside, swimming with them. After all, I'd been hanging out with the Seven for a good part of my growing years, if you get my drift?

Over the years, whenever I had time off from my tours, I had taken to coming into London without telling anyone. It was much simpler that way. For me, for them... Particularly, for Edward. He doesn't need a reminder about just what had been done to us during the incident. And I am better off not having to re-live what had happened every time I run into him. No, this is best.

I keep in touch with Edward and the rest of the Seven with the occasional snail mail letter. I haven't told them the details of what I've been up to, but have shared just enough in the letters that they know I am alive. Of course, I haven't revealed where I am based either. Just a precaution, so none of them have any chance of finding me, in case they are tempted.

And maybe it had been cowardly of me not to tell them face-to-face of my decision to join the army, but in all honesty, until I'd walked out of that warehouse, I hadn't been sure about it either. Not until I had spent half that night walking about the city, had I realized what I needed to do.

The Army was exactly the right place for me. A space where I could dedicate myself to a cause bigger than me. A way to forget my past, subsume my needs and wants in favor of the greater good, a means of not having to think but simply follow orders, to do as I was told, make sure I had the backs of my fellow soldiers. It had been better for me than I had expected... My years of participating in extreme sports stood me in good stead. I didn't take risks unless they were well-calculated ones, and it turns out, I have a deadly eye for shooting. Not to mention my proclivity for being a hacker meant I was exceptionally good at interrogating and getting information from enemy soliders. Everything was going well, until I was captured and became a POW for two years.

Unsurprisingly, that triggered the demons in my mind to come roaring back, and once I was discharged from the army, I found I craved silence. The chance to simply live in the moment while I cherish my solitude.

I found myself an apartment in Madrid, spend my waking hours either working out at the gym or teaching self-defense classes at the local community center. As long as I keep moving, I can keep the ghosts in my mind at bay. The ghosts that have haunted me since the incident, and which had only gotten worse when I had been captured and held as a prisoner of war. They had tortured me, to unlock the secrets I had carried inside my head, but I hadn't broken. Turns out, even a war enemy cannot torture you as much as those bastards who had kidnapped us.

Should I be grateful that I had faced, possibly, the worst test of my life so early on? Or should I simply look forward, and try to move on from what had happened to me? Can I do that?

"Heathrow Express will be ready to depart from platform two in five minutes. Passengers, please make your way to the platform now."

I square my shoulders, heave my backpack over my shoulder and rise to my feet, when a peal of laughter reaches me. The hair on the back of my neck rises. I whip my head around, try to place the source of the laugh.

A crowd of men pass me by. One of them claps the other on the back of his head and the rest of them chortle in amusement. They remind me of the Seven, of how it had been when I was one of them.

I had made the choice to leave for the army, at the same time that Edward had decided to become a priest. We'd gone our separate ways, and that's fine. This way, neither of us had to bear the burden of being reminded of the incident. This way, we could each find our own path in life... Or what passes for that.

Another peal of laughter cuts through the thoughts in my head. Only when my feet hit the ground, do I realize that I have stood up and am moving forward, following that sound of laughter. I sweep my gaze across a gaggle of girls talking to each other; no, she's not among them.

I brush past them, catch sight of a family walking ahead of me. The father and mother are followed by two girls. One of them wears a dress that falls to just below her knees. Her auburn hair flows past her shoulders. A beam of light bounces off of the rippling locks, highlighting the red in them and haloing her head. She's not very tall, maybe five feet four inches, at the most. Her curves are highlighted by her outfit, enough to indicate that she is a woman. She's not that old... Not that young either. Maybe seventeen — or eighteen?

She turns her face to speak to her sister and I catch a glimpse of her profile. The upturned nose, the curve of her lips, the creamy skin that glows in the late afternoon light. She throws her head back and laughs, and my heart begins to pound in my chest. Sweat beads my palms and I wipe them on my jeans. Shit, what is this reaction to her? I don't know her, have not even properly met her, yet something inside me insists that I know her. That she is the same as the little girl I'd seen all those years ago at that pub.

The girl who I have tried hard not to think about, for in my mind, she had stayed little. But she is all grown up. Still younger than me, but at least, I don't feel like a perv anymore as I gaze at her across the distance.

A few men in business suits walk toward me. They hide the family from sight. I dodge around them, past a woman clinging to a man who seems reluctant to leave her.

Ahead of them, the family piles inside a car and I hasten my pace, until I am almost sprinting. Can it be her? It has to be her. The girl I'd gotten a glimpse of so many years ago. That laughter is the same, yet throatier. This is crazy.

A mother and her son walk toward me. The kid's ball slips from his grasp. It bounces toward me, heading for the tracks. He cries out, races for his toy, but his mother pulls him back. I glance up at the girl in the distance, down at the toy, then jump forward to stop it with my foot. I scoop it up and toss it at the boy. He catches it and his face breaks into a grin, "Thanks Mister." His delight showcases a big gap-toothed smile.

I nod, glance up toward the compartment where the family had disappeared. I jog toward it when, with a beeping sound, all of the doors of the train slide shut. *Shit, shit, shit.* I race forward, but I am too late. The train starts to move.

Bloody hell. I draw in a breath, drag my fingers through my hair. Goddamnit, I lost her a second time. Will I ever see her again?

To find out what happens next read Billionaire's Sins HERE

Get Sinclair and Summer's story in The Billionaire's Fake Wife HERE

Want to be the first to find out about my NEWEST release? Join my newsletter HERE

Read an excerpt from Billionaire's Sins...

Ava

"Each blossom still blooms in its field; each child still clutches your hand; each friend still lingers in your heart. And that...is where time goes."

I glance at the words I've scrawled out in my diary.

My heart stutters. The hair on my forearms rises. Time. Why am I so obsessed with time? I am only nineteen; I have my entire life in front of me. So why do I often ponder how fast time goes by? How it can all be over in a matter of minutes... Blink, and it's gone. A mother playing with her son as an infant one second; the next, he's all grown up and she's shooting a movie with him as her subject. The son, who is the mirror image of her first and only love, the man she fell for, her soulmate...who turned out not to be. And now she has him... The son, who is the image of the father. Stop it... All these thoughts that meld and flow and turn my brain to mush. Even Twilight was more cheerful than this.

I hear a splash from the pool, and glance around from my perch on the chair in the far corner of the pool area. I am at my friend Summer's townhouse in Primrose Hill. It's February and freezing in London. Which is why I had grabbed my book and my blanket, then crawled over to the far end of the pool area. I'd hidden behind the wide trunk of the oak-tree, then settled down to write.

People hate the cold. Me? I thrive on it. Darkness is my friend, my companion. It clothes me, hides me from the sight of the world, like this blanket that I've wrapped around myself. If I look down, I can see the slope of Primrose Hill fall away below, the grass an undulating carpet that stretches down to the canal. This early in the day, it is quiet, except for a few joggers... And the man who'd dived into the pool and is now swimming laps.

From my hiding place, I can see his massive shoulders flex as he cuts through the water. He propels forward, leaving ripples in his wake. He's moving so fast, he's almost a blur as his powerful arms slice through the water. He hits one end of the swimming pool, then pushes away and begins to swim toward the other side. He zips forward, flings out an arm, thrusts the other back so his body shoots ahead. He lunges onward, keeps going until he hits the other edge of the pool, then turns back. I watch as he does five more laps of the pool... Hell, is he training for a triathlon or something? My entire body hurts, thinking of the punishment he's putting himself through. What the hell is he trying to prove anyway?

He hits the edge of the pool, throws his arms over the rim and holds on. Then he presses his hands down on the ground, hauls himself up. He pitches his leg up and over. The corded muscles of his thigh tauten as he raises himself up tand over the side. Water streams down from his sculpted chest, the cut planes of his back, and pours down the sides of his thighs. He raises his arms, throws back his head and stretches. For a second, he stands poised. The first rays of the sun hit his skin, and he seems to sparkle. My throat dries. All of my nerve endings pop. Moisture pools in my core. A shiver runs down my spine.

He turns, giving me a full-frontal view and I draw in a breath. I saw him at my friend Karina's wedding, a few weeks ago. Only difference, he had more clothes on…and he wasn't this wet. Nor was I—ha! Nor did he have his thick hair slicked back to outline the contours of his scalp. Nor did the hollows under his cheekbones seem this prominent. I trace my gaze down his hooked nose to his thin upper lip, made all the more pronounced by his full lower lip, which seems soft, pouty enough for me to sink my teeth into and suck. My belly clenches. My core softens. I squeeze my thighs together, watch as he moves toward the deckchair and picks up a towel. He drags it down his massive chest, across that ripped stomach, down the crotch of his black swimsuit, which outline what he's packing. I bite down on the inside of my cheek. Is that man packing or what?

Is he some kind of athlete? He has that strength and confidence that comes with someone who works a physical profession. Or else, he trains a lot. As evidenced by this morning's work out.

He loops the towel around his neck, straightens, then meets my gaze.

I pull back. "Shit, shit, shit." Did he see me? Of course, he spotted me. He seems like the kind of man who wouldn't miss a thing in his surroundings.

Go on, get out there and wave at him or something. Tell him 'Hi.'

"Hi." I wiggle my fingers in the air in his general direction, too embarrassed to look that way again.

"Hello, there." A gruff voice sounds above me and I yelp. My heart pounds in my chest as I glance up, straight at eye-level with his gorgeous crotch—now covered by his pants. He'd managed to pull those on before heading over, apparently. Not that it does anything to hide, but rather, reveals the gargantuan proportions of whatever it is that it encloses.

Jeez, get your mind out of the gutter, bitch.

I raise my gaze, and hell, if the view doesn't get even more serious. Dense muscles, packed one on top of the other, moving, slipping, sliding as he draws in a breath. An intricate design inches over one shoulder, and damn, if I don't want to jump up and peek around to find out how it continues across his back.

He folds his arms across his chest and his biceps bulge.

Heat sears my blood. My thighs clench.

I tilt my head back, and further back. The sun chooses that moment to shine on him again, shadowing his features. This guy is a sun trap; that's for sure. The golden glow folds about him, caresses him, so sparks of amber flare in the air around him. I blink, and his face comes into view. Dark close-cropped hair slicked back from the water. His eyes are golden...amber with a hint of black in their depths. Like he has secrets which he holds close to his chest. Thick eyelashes that sweep down over high cheekbones you could cut yourself on. I curl my fingers into fists and my nails dig into my flesh.

A scar mars the expanse of his left cheek, and somehow that only heightens how perfect the rest of his face is.

"You okay?" He tilts his head.

"Of course." My voice cracks and I clear my throat. "Why wouldn't I be?"

"You seem like you saw something...unexpected?"

"Uh, you're not a vampire, are you?"

He blinks, then chuckles. A full-throated, deep reverberation that sucker-punches me in the gut. My thighs tremble. My toes curl. I watch as those full lips of his quirk.

"I'm Edward." He holds out his hand.

"Wha—" I gape, "you're kidding me, right?"

He frowns. "Excuse me?"

"Your...your name," I choke out. "It can't be Edward."

"I am not following..." His cultured tone carries a note of warning, which I ignore.

"I mean, you can't be called Edward. Who put you up to this? Was it Isla?" Only she knows about my slightly stalkerish obsession with Edward, from Twilight, and surely, she wouldn't tell the others, right?

"Ah." The wrinkles on his forehead dissipate. "You're Isla's friend?"

I hold out my hand, "Ava."

"Ava?" He frowns.

He touches my hand and the rest of the words dry in my throat. Goosebumps flare on my skin. His gaze widens and the planes of his chest twitch. Did he feel that shock of the impact as well? I try to pull back my hand but he holds onto it.

"Why are you hiding, Eve?"

"I'm not," I scowl. "and that's not my name."

"It suits you better," he tilts his head, "and you haven't answered my question yet."

"Which one?"

"What are you doing here?"

"I came here to write," I bite the inside of my cheek, "only... I heard the splashing in the pool and I turned around and spotted you swimming.

"And you watched?" His lips curl in a hint of a smirk.

I glance away. "I, uh, may have peeked a bit."

"Did you like what you saw?"

I jerk my head in his direction, to find him watching me closely. His expression is one of curiosity, like I am some kind of lab specimen whose responses he is clocking in a clinical way. The hair on the back of my neck rises. I want to glance away, break the connection with this man, but I can't. My pulse rate ratchets up. Despite the chill in the morning, my palms begin to sweat. I clear my gaze, force the words out, "Wh....why Eve?"

"You know why." He peruses my features. "And you haven't answered the question."

"Do I?" My heart begins to race. "And what question?"

"You know the answer to both." He folds his arms across his chest and his impressive biceps bulge. Heat blooms between my legs and I resist the urge to rub my thighs together.

"I'm not sure what you're referring to," I say stiffly, "and no, I don't find you attractive."

His grin widens, and the impact of that smile... Oh, my. His teeth sparkle against the tan of his skin, his features brighten, the charisma pours off of him, and honestly, I can't glance away. I take in the gleam in his eyes, the hair on his forehand drying and already curling a little.

I blink. "Aren't you cold?"

The breeze picks up, and a strand of hair whips across my face.

He releases my hand, only to lean down and push the hair aside. Goosebumps pop on my skin. My stomach trembles and my heart begins to race. I watch as his gaze holds mine, as the pupils of his eyes dilate. His nostrils flare, and he straightens. "I'd better be going. Sinclair's expecting me for breakfast."

"Oh, that's right. Me too." I'd promised Summer I'd join them for breakfast. I jump up, and the movement brings me close to him. The heat of his body slams into my chest and my throat dries. I stare up at him, as he glares down his nose. Something like anger steals across his features, before he schools all expression from his face. A strange sensation grips my chest. I draw in a breath and the oxygen rushes to my head. Shit, when had I forgotten to breathe? He steps back, and the cold air rushes in. I shiver.

He pivots, walking toward the pool house. I take in the tattoo of the snake that crawls diagonally across his back. Whoa! That's one mean-ass tattoo. It's as spectacular as it is unexpected against the much paler skin of his back. The forked tongue of the snake is thick in girth, and within it are etched tribal signs that I can't decipher. The edge of it flows over his shoulder, which is what I must have seen earlier. The scales on the snake are patterned in color and the triangular head has slitted eyes which seem to follow me as I jump to my feet, then tug the blanket around me, hold my book close and follow.

"Hold on," I protest, "your legs are too long."

He slows his pace and I catch up.

"So, you are a friend of Sinclair's?"

He nods.

"You're one of the Seven, aren't you?" I peer up into his face, "I saw you at Arpad and Karina's wedding."

His jaw hardens. Now what did I say for him to seem angry?

"Surely, you remember?" I mutter. "Didn't you notice me?"

"I don't notice every girl who crosses my path."

I blink, then pause my steps, "Now, that's not fair. I could have sworn that you saw me there. Besides, I am not a girl."

He pulls forward, and I run to catch up. "Did you hear what I said?" I demand. "I am not a—"

"Girl." He stops so quickly that I bump into him. The scent of chlorine, and under that, the fresh-cut grass scent of him teases my nostrils. I draw in a breath, filling my lungs with his earthy essence. Moisture pools in my center and my nerve-endings seem to fire all at once. Why the hell does he have to smell so utterly delectable?

He pivots to face me and the heat of his body seems to turn up a notch. Does this man have a furnace under his skin, or what?

He looks me up and down. "What are you then?" he asks.

"What—" I blink.

"You said you are not a girl, so what are you?"

I tip up my chin. "A woman." I square my shoulders. "I am a woman."

"And I..." He squares his shoulders, "I am sworn to celibacy..."

Edward

"Excuse me?" She gapes. "What...what did you say?"

Shit, what the hell had I been thinking? Why had I blurted that out? Because I am attracted to her... There, the simple truth. I've never been so affected by a woman as I have been since I first saw her at City Hall when she'd appeared next to the bride...and my world had reduced, shrunk down to her eyes, her mouth... That aura of her which shines so brightly, so purely. So innocent. How old is she anyway?

How could I have known then, that she would be trouble? That every single thing I'd sworn off, every vow I had taken... All of it would culminate in this test. This...trial that God has selected for me. And I cannot give in. No way. Not by all that I hold dear to me. There is space for only one attraction, one relationship, one complete obsession. To the One Above.

So, I had taken the easy way out. The cowardly way, you say? Maybe, but it is better to be upfront about what I am. I need to be clear that there can never be anything between us...

Hell, why am I even thinking along those lines? Not that she seems unduly affected by me, but that spark of awareness between us... I hadn't imagined that. Or the way her pupils had dilated, or how she had leaned in to me, how she'd sniffed me. She says she's not a girl anymore... but I beg to differ. She's all female, all coltish limbs and a translucent skin that reflects whatever she is feeling.

"I have taken a vow." I step back from her. "I have promised to live a celibate life. I have completely given my life to Christ and the people I have been called to serve."

I turn away from her, head for the clothes that I'd placed on the pool-chair.

The hair on the nape of my neck prickles.

I glance over my shoulder to find her staring at me. Her gaze runs down my back, then back to my face, as I snatch up my shirt and shrug into it.

"I... I don't understand."

"Me neither." I grab my towel, then head for the guesthouse that I occupy whenever I stay over at the Sterlings', which isn't often. But when I'd wanted to leave yesterday, the rest of the Seven wouldn't hear of it. With Arpad getting married, it means all of us are now hitched... Well, except me... And Baron. I stiffen. Why the hell am I thinking of him? The friend who'd turned his back on us and left. Not that he hasn't been in touch. He's communicated through snail mail, writing on occasion, like when Damian was hesitant about getting married to Julia. Or when there is a specific investment that Sinner or Saint aren't sure about, though how he knows this is beyond me. The two of them run 7A Investments, one of the leading financial services firms in the country. Between them, they've managed to invest our money such that we'll be living off the wealth created for this entire lifetime. Not that I am going to touch a penny of it.

My investments go toward FOK Media, aka Full of Kindness Media, the non-profit that the Seven set up to finance upcoming talent in return for a portion of their earnings. I'd also put money toward my own trust that supports the most vulnerable and those in need.

As for myself, I stay in a small two-bedroom home, owned by the parish I am devoted to serving. The place where I need to return before things get further out of hand. It had been wrong to approach her in the first place. I'd seen her watching me, had recognized her—Of course, I had. I couldn't have missed her—and then I had approached her. I should have walked away, but I couldn't resist. I had to see her once more. And now I have to atone for the sinful thoughts I entertained.

I clench my fists at my sides.

"Wait." Her footsteps approach me, and I increase my pace.

I cannot be alone with her, not for one more second.

"What are you trying to tell me, Edward?"

I reach the guesthouse, twist open the door and step in. I turn to find her hesitating at the entrance and beckon her in.

She hesitates and I tilt my head. "Come on, I have something to show you."

"You do?" Her forehead furrows.

"You need to see this."

She blows out a breath and follows me. I head inside, to the bedroom, take my collar from where I'd placed it on the bedstead. I slip it on, then turn to find her poised at the doorway.

Her face pales; her jaw drops.

"You're a...a—"

"Priest." I nod.

"B...but," she opens and shuts her mouth, "you weren't wearing a collar at the wedding yesterday."

"I'm a diocesan priest. I wear the collar when I have anything pastoral to do. I don't usually wear it when out with friends."

"I see." She shrugs off her blanket, folds it over her arm. Her gaze skitters away. "I knew it was too good to be true. Of course, it is." She retreats into the living room, drops the blanket and her book on the couch and begins to pace. "I mean, just once, things couldn't be easy for me, right? Everything has to be complicated. Just this once, couldn't things have worked out the way they do for everyone else? Of course, not." She throws up her hands. "This is not fair, not fair at all."

"Are you..." I follow her as she stomps back-forth-back, across the length of the floor of the living room. "Are you talking to yourself?"

"Shh." She turns to me and frowns. "I'm trying to figure this out."

"By talking aloud?"

"Hey, don't mock it until you try it. Did you know talking to yourself helps you organize your thoughts?" She shoves her purple-tipped hair back from her face.

Who dyes their hair purple? Ava does, that's who.

"According to psychologists, talking out loud to yourself helps you clarify your thoughts," she mumbles. "It helps to figure out what's important, and firm up any decisions you're contemplating."

"Ah," I allow my lips to tip up, "and what decision are you contemplating right now?"

She flushes. "I am not sure you want to know."

"Don't I?"

*T*O *FIND OUT WHAT HAPPENS NEXT GET* B*ILLIONAIRE'S* S*INS* **HERE**

G*ET* S*INCLAIR AND* S*UMMER'S STORY IN* T*HE* B*ILLIONAIRE'S* F*AKE* W*IFE* **HERE**

W*ANT TO BE THE FIRST TO FIND OUT ABOUT MY* **NEWEST** *RELEASE*? J*OIN MY NEWSLETTER* **HERE**

R*EAD AN EXCERPT FROM MAFIA KING*

Karma

"Morn came and went—and came, and brought no day…"

Tears prick the back of my eyes. Goddamn Byron. Crept up on me when I am at my weakest. Not that I am a poetry addict, by any measure, but words are my jam.

The one consolation I have, that when everything else in the world is wrong, I can turn to them, and they'll be there, friendly steady, waiting with open arms. And this particular poem had laced my blood, crawled into my gut when I'd first read it. Darkness had folded into me like an insidious snake that raises its head when I least expect it. Like now. I'd managed to give my bodyguard the slip and veered off my usual running route to reach *Waterlow Park*.

I look out on the still sleeping city of London, from the grassy slope of the expanse. Somewhere out there the Mafia was hunting me, apparently.

I purse my lips, close my eyes. Silence. The rustle of the wind between the leaves, the faint tinkle of the water from the nearby spring.

I could be the last person on this planet, alone, unsung, bound for the grave.

Ugh! Stop. Right there. I drag the back of my hand across my nose. Try it again, focus, get the words out, one after the other, like the steps of my sorry life.

"*Morn came and went—and came, and brought no day…*" My voice breaks. "Bloody, asinine, hell." I dig my fingers into the grass and grab a handful and fling it out. Again. From the top. I open my eyes, focus on a spot in the distance.

"Morn came and went—and came, and…."

"…brought no day."

I whip my head around. His profile fills my line of sight. Dark hair combed back by a ruthless hand that booked no measure.

My throat dries.

Hooked nose, thin upper lip, a fleshy lower lip, that hints at hidden desires. Heat. Lust. The sensuous scrape of that whiskered jaw over my innermost places. Across my inner thigh, reaching toward that core of me that throbs, clenches, melts to feel the stab of his tongue, the thrust of his hardness as he impales me, takes me, makes me his.

"*Of this their desolation; and all hearts*
Were chill'd into a selfish prayer for light.."

Sweat beads my palm; the hairs on my nape rise. "Who are you?"

He stares ahead, his lips moving,

"*Forests were set on fire—but hour by hour*
They fell and faded—and the crackling trunks
Extinguish'd with a crash—and all was black."

I swallow, squeeze my thighs together. Moisture gathers in my core. How can I be wet by the mere cadence of this stranger's voice?

I spring up to my feet.

"Sit down."

His voice is unhurried, lazy even, his spine erect. The cut of his black jacket stretches across the width of his massive shoulders. His hair… I was mistaken. There are strands of dark gold woven between the darkness that pours down to brush the nape of his neck. My fingers tingle. My scalp itches.

I take in a breath and my lungs burn.

This man, he's sucked all the oxygen in this open space, as if he owns it, the master of all he surveys. The master of me. My death. My life. A shiver ladders its way up my spine. *Get away, get away now, while you still can.*

I take a step back.

"I won't ask again."

Ask. Command. Force me to do as he wants. He'll have me on my back, bent over, on the side, over him, under him, he'll surround me, overwhelm me, pin me down with the force of his personality. His charisma, his larger-than-life essence that will crush everything else out of me and I... I'll love it.

"No."

"Yes."

A fact. A statement of intent, spoken aloud. So true. So real. Too real. Too much. Too fast. All of my nightmares... my dreams come to life. Everything I've wanted is here in front of me. I'll die a thousand deaths before he'll be done with me... and then, will I be reborn? For him. For me. For myself. I live first and foremost to be the woman I am... am meant to be.

"You want to run?"

No.

No.

I nod my head

He turns his head and all of the breath leaves my lungs. Blue eyes, cerulean, dark like the morning skies, deep like the nighttime, hidden corners, secrets that I don't dare uncover. He'll destroy me, have my heart, and break it so casually.

My throat burns. A boiling sensation squeezes my chest.

"Go then, my beauty, fly. You have until I count to five. If I catch you, you are mine."

"If you don't?"

"Then I'll come after you, stalk your every living moment, possess your nightmares, and steal you away in the dead of midnight, and then..."

I draw in a shuddering breath; liquid heat drips from between my legs. "Then?" I whisper.

"Then, I'll ensure you'll never belong to anyone else, you'll never see the light of day again, for your every breath, your every waking second, your thoughts, your actions... and all of your words, every single last one, will belong to me." He peels back his lips, and his teeth glint in the first rays of the morning light. "Only me." He straightens to his feet, and rises, and rises.

He is massive. A beast. A monster who always gets his way. My guts churn. My toes curl. Something primal inside me insists I hold my own. I cannot give in to him. Cannot let him win whatever this is. I need to stake my ground in some form. *Say something. Anything. Show him you're not afraid of him.*

"Why?" I tilt my head back, all the way back. "Why are you doing this?"

He tilts his head, his ears almost canine in the way they are silhouetted against his profile.

"Is it because you can? Is it a... a..." I blink, "a debt of some kind?"

He stills.

"My father. This is about how he betrayed the Mafia, right? You're one of them?"

All expression is wiped clean of his face, and I know then I am right. My past... Why does it always catch up with me? *You can run, but you can never hide.*

"Tick-tock, Beauty." He angles his body and his shoulders shut out the sight of the sun, the dawn skies, the horizon, the city in the distance, the whisper of the grass, the trees, the rustle of the leaves... All of it fades, and leaves me and him. Us. *Run.*

"Five." He jerks his chin. Straightens the cuffs of his sleeves.

My knees wobble.

"Four."

My heart hammers in my chest. I should go. Leave. But my feet are welded to this earth. This piece of land where we first met. What am I, but a speck in the larger scheme of things? To be hurt. To be forgotten. To be brought to the edge of climax and taken without an ounce of retribution. To be punished... by him.

"Three." He thrusts out his chest, widens his stance, every muscle in his body relaxed. "Two."

I swallow. The pulse beats at my temples. My blood thrums.

"One."

TO FIND OUT WHAT HAPPENS NEXT READ KARMA AND MICHAEL BYRON'S STORY HERE

CLAIM YOUR FREE CONTEMPORARY ROMANCE BOOK. CLICK HERE

CLAIM YOUR FREE PARANORMAL ROMANCE BOOK HERE

MORE BOOKS BY L. STEELE

MORE BOOKS BY LAXMI

CLAIM YOUR FREE CONTEMPORARY ROMANCE BOOK. CLICK HERE

CLAIM YOUR FREE PARANORMAL ROMANCE BOOK HERE

FOLLOW ME ON BOOKBUB

FOLLOW ON GOODREADS

FOLLOW ME ON TIKTOK

FOLLOW MY PINTEREST BOARDS

FOLLOW ME ON FB

FOLLOW ME ON INSTAGRAM

JOIN MY SECRET FACEBOOK READER GROUP; I AM DYING TO MEET YOU!

READ MY BOOKS HERE

FREE BOOKS

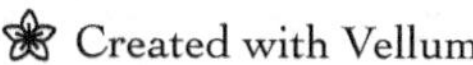 Created with Vellum

www.ingramcontent.com/pod-product-compliance
Lightning Source LLC
Chambersburg PA
CBHW071817190726
48292CB00008B/2883